Marshmallow Mystery

Candy Fairies

Marshmallow Mystery

HELEN PERELMAN

ILLUSTRATED BY
ERICA-JANE WATERS

ALADDIN
NEW YORK   LONDON   TORONTO   SYDNEY   NEW DELHI

ALADDIN

An imprint of Simon & Schuster Children's Publishing Division

1230 Avenue of the Americas, New York, NY 10020

First Aladdin paperback edition January 2014

Text copyright © 2014 by Helen Perelman Bernstein

Illustrations copyright © 2014 by Erica-Jane Waters

All rights reserved, including the right of reproduction in whole or in part in any form.

ALADDIN is a trademark of Simon & Schuster, Inc., and related logo is a registered trademark of Simon & Schuster, Inc.

Also available in an Aladdin hardcover edition.

For information about special discounts for bulk purchases, please contact Simon & Schuster Special Sales at 1-866-506-1949 or business@simonandschuster.com.

The Simon & Schuster Speakers Bureau can bring authors to your live event.

For more information or to book an event contact the Simon & Schuster Speakers Bureau at 1-866-248-3049 or visit our website at www.simonspeakers.com.

Designed by Karina Granda

The text of this book was set in Berthold Baskerville Book.

Manufactured in the United States of America 0416 OFF

2 4 6 8 10 9 7 5 3

Library of Congress Control Number 2013953375

ISBN 978-1-4424-5301-2 (pbk)

ISBN 978-1-4424-6500-8 (hc)

ISBN 978-1-4424-5302-9 (eBook)

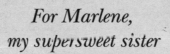

For Marlene,
my supersweet sister

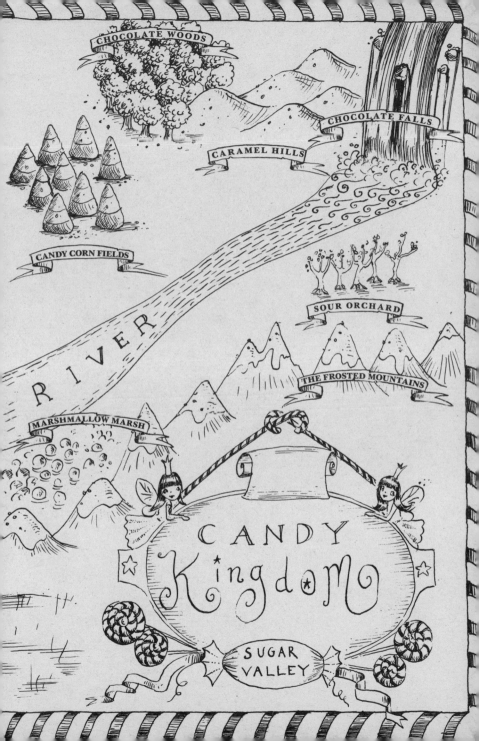

Contents

CHAPTER
1

Peppermint Problem

Raina the Gummy Fairy was enjoying a quiet afternoon in Gummy Forest. The sun was beginning to set, and she was feeding the gummy fish. Twice a day she sprinkled the flavor flakes into Gummy Lake. Raina loved taking care of the animals who lived in Gummy Forest.

All of a sudden a loud voice startled her.

"Raina!" shouted Dash the Mint Fairy.

Dash whizzed down to the ground as if she were in a race. She nearly knocked Raina over when she landed.

"I am so happy to find you!" Dash cried.

"Whoa!" Raina exclaimed. She stumbled backward as Dash hugged her. When Raina saw her friend's face, she gasped. "What's wrong?"

Dash pushed a lock of her blond hair out of her face. Her small silver wings were beating superfast. "I really need to talk to you," she said, panting.

Dash was one of the fastest fairies in Sugar Valley. Raina could tell that Dash had just made the trip to Gummy Forest in record time.

"Okay, okay," Raina said. "Slow down. There's no race today." She smiled. No one loved a race more than her friend Dash.

Dash put her hands on her knees and took a few deep breaths. She took an extra-long breath in and out before she spoke. "It's Mallow," Dash finally said.

"The frosted white owl in Marshmallow Marsh?" Raina asked. She looked very concerned. She put her feeding bucket down. "Is he all right?"

Dash shook her head. "I am not sure," she said. Dash's blue eyes were wide with concern. "He was acting very strange when I saw him."

"What do you mean?" Raina asked.

"I think that he may be hiding something," Dash replied.

 3

Raina looked at Dash carefully. Mallow was an owl, so he spent his days sleeping and his nights exploring Sugar Valley. "Wait a sweet second," Raina said. "What were you doing in the marsh so late at night?"

"That is what makes this all so strange," Dash told her. "I just saw Mallow! In the *afternoon*! And he wasn't sleeping." She took another deep breath before continuing. "I was getting some marshmallow frosting for my racing sled, and there he was!"

Raina looked up at the darkening sky. "Well, it is close to nighttime now," she said. "Soon it will be Sun Dip. Maybe he was getting up a little early?"

Dash leaped up in the air. "I don't think so. He didn't look like he had slept at all. He wasn't very chatty, either," she said. "You know Mallow loves to tell stories. But just now he rushed off and barely had time for a quick hello."

"Let's sit down over here," Raina said. She guided Dash over to the dock by the lake and they sat down on the edge.

"I'm not just upset by seeing Mallow," Dash said. "There's something else that's worrying me."

Raina watched Dash carefully. "What else?"

"Well," Dash said, "before I was at the marsh, I noticed broken candy canes in Peppermint Grove along the Chocolate River shoreline." She tilted her head. "Do you think that might be part of the reason Mallow is acting so strange?" She wrapped her arms around herself. "Do you

think maybe there is something or someone haunting the marsh?"

"You sound like you've been reading some Lupa stories," Raina said, smiling. Raina had lent Dash a book about the brave Candy Fairy explorer Lupa. Lupa stories were full of adventure—and sometimes a little spooky.

"Maybe," Dash admitted. "I love Lupa mysteries."

Raina reached for the Fairy Code Book in her bag. "Lupa mysteries are good," she said. "But the Fairy Code Book usually has the answers."

A smile spread across Dash's face. "I knew you'd know just the right page to turn to in the Fairy Code Book," she said. "That's why I came here. You always think of some story to help figure out a problem. No one knows the Fairy Code Book better than you!"

Raina blushed. "Well, the Fairy Code Book is special. It holds the history and secrets of the Candy Fairies." She flipped open the thick book. "If I am remembering correctly," Raina said, "I think there's a similar story about broken chocolate branches in Chocolate Woods that might help explain Mallow's behavior."

"You always remember correctly!" Dash exclaimed. "I think that is one of the reasons why Princess Lolli trusted you to look after the Fairy Code Book. You read the book more than anyone!"

Raina laughed. "Maybe," she said. She turned the pages slowly.

"I bet Princess Lolli thought for a long time about which fairy she would give that book to," Dash went on. "You should feel very proud. It's not like the ruler of Candy Kingdom would let just anyone have that special book."

"I am honored," Raina said. She continued searching. Then she pointed to the open page in front of her. "Ah, just what I thought!"

Dash leaned over and stared at the page Raina was pointing at. There was a drawing of Mogu, the salty troll who lived under a bridge in Black Licorice Swamp. The troll and his little Chuchies loved to steal the Candy Fairies' candy.

"Oh no," Dash moaned. "You think Mogu is involved?"

"Maybe. Here's the story I was thinking

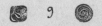

about," Raina said. She began to read a tale about Mogu and a chocolate bunny quarreling near Chocolate Woods. There were broken chocolate branches and there was missing candy. Raina stopped reading and looked up at Dash. "Have you noticed anything missing in Peppermint Grove?"

"Oh, peppermint sticks!" Dash said. "I am

not sure. But I wonder if Mogu is also to blame for Mallow's odd behavior."

Raina closed the book. "Sadly, Mogu is usually involved in these salty times," she said with a sigh. She slid the book back into her bag and picked up the feeding bucket.

"I haven't seen Mogu at all," Dash said. "But I will keep watch. And take a careful look at the mint crops."

"Keep checking on Mallow," Raina advised.

"I will," Dash said.

"Great," Raina replied. "Poor, sweet Mallow. He is such a gentle and wise owl. I hope that he is all right."

"I want to help him," Dash said. "He has always been so kind to me. When I am training for a race, at night he leaves a marshmallow

treat for me at the finish line so I can have it on my first run down the mountain."

"Sweet," Raina said. Dash often trained on the trails of the Frosted Mountains that wound down to Marshmallow Marsh. Dash was an expert sled racer. Raina reached over and gave Dash a tight hug. "You are a good friend, Dash," she said.

"You are too," Dash told her. "Thanks for that story about the chocolate branches! If Mogu is bothering Mallow, I want to help."

Just then there was a rustling in the gummy branches. Dash leaped up in the air. "Sweet peppermint!" she cried.

Raina smiled. "It's only Blue Belle," she said. "Come here, sweetie." Raina reached out to the small gummy cub.

"Blue Belle," Dash said, "you scared me."

Blue Belle giggled and bowed her head bashfully.

"I think Blue Belle wants her food," Raina explained. She slipped her some flavor flakes, and the cub settled down to eat.

"Bye, Blue Belle! Bye, Raina!" Dash said as she took off toward Peppermint Grove.

"I'll see you soon at Red Licorice Lake for Sun Dip!" Raina called after her.

As Dash flew away, Raina hoped that Mallow's problem was just a quick quarrel with Mogu, but she wasn't sure that Mallow's behavior was due to just Mogu's hunting down candy. She tried to shake off her concern and went back to her peaceful task of feeding the gummy fish.

CHAPTER 2

Supersour

On the red sugar sand beach of Red Licorice Lake, Raina waited for her friends to gather for Sun Dip. This was her favorite time of day. The sky was a dark lavender and the sun was low in the sky. As her friends arrived, Raina wondered what was keeping Dash. Dash was *never* late.

"What's wrong, Raina?" Berry asked. The Fruit Fairy settled down next to Raina on a blanket. Her sparkling fruit-chew hair clips were lined up neatly in her hair. Berry was the most fashionable of all the fairies.

"Dash isn't here yet," Raina said to Berry. "She came to Gummy Forest before Sun Dip, and she was worried about Mallow."

"I beat her here?" Berry said, surprised. She looked around. "Lickin' lollipops! This must be a first!"

Melli the Caramel Fairy and Cocoa the Chocolate Fairy moved in closer. Raina saw concern on their faces.

"What's wrong with Mallow?" Melli asked.

"First Dash said that Mallow was acting odd and wouldn't talk to her. It was the

middle of the afternoon, and he was awake when he should have been sleeping. Then she told me that she had spotted broken candy canes along Chocolate River," Raina explained.

"Hot chocolate!" Cocoa exclaimed.

"I found a story in the Fairy Code Book about Mogu and broken chocolate branches," Raina went on. "We thought Mogu might be the cause of Mallow's problems."

"Poor Mallow," Melli said. "He is such a sweet owl. I hope he's all right."

Raina looked off toward Marshmallow Marsh. "I know," she said. "Maybe Dash is talking to Mallow now." Raina drew her breath in quickly. "I hope she's not talking to Mogu alone!"

"Raina, what made you think of Mogu?" Melli asked.

Cocoa laughed. "Of course Raina remembered a story from the Fairy Code Book."

Raina could tell her friends were joking with her. She knew that everyone thought she had memorized the large book from cover to cover, she had read it so many times.

Cocoa spread her wings. "Oh, I hope it wasn't Mogu," she said. "Princess Lolli and Prince Scoop are not at Candy Castle and can't help us. They're visiting Prince Scoop's family in Ice Cream Isles."

"This could be supersticky," Melli mumbled.

"Don't dip your wings in syrup yet," Berry said. "Let's wait to hear what Dash has to say."

The light in the sky grew dimmer and

darker. Finally, Raina spotted Dash's silver wings.

"Dash!" Raina cried. "Where have you been? Are you okay?"

Dash flew down to the blanket her friends were on. "I tried to catch Mallow," she told the fairies. "I sat by the hollow tree he sleeps in and waited and waited. I thought maybe if I asked him about Mogu, he would feel comfortable telling me if something salty had happened."

"But Mallow didn't come out?" Cocoa asked.

"That's strange," Raina said.

"Maybe he didn't want to talk," Berry said.

Dash shot Berry a minty glare.

"It's possible," Berry said, shrugging.

"Or maybe he is in trouble," Dash said. "He was awake in Marshmallow Marsh before

Sun Dip today, and that has never happened before."

"Is there a story in the Fairy Code Book about Mallow, or even another owl in Sugar Valley?" Melli asked Raina.

"There's a story about everything in the Fairy Code Book," Cocoa said. "Right, Raina?"

Raina shook her head. "Not always," she said. "Mallow up before Sun Dip is not something a fairy hears every day."

Dash reached out for a chocolate treat from Cocoa's basket. "And don't forget, the book has every single candy recipe too," she said. She rubbed her stomach. "Maybe that is why I can't read the book very often. I would get too hungry!"

The fairies all laughed. Dash had one of

the largest appetites in Sugar Valley.

"Maybe we should check the Fairy Code Book again," Melli suggested. "There might be another story that explains what happened today."

Raina reached into her bag. Her face turned as white as fresh peppermint. "The Fairy Code Book!"

"Yes," Dash said, staring at the selection of chocolates. "What does the book say?" She popped another chocolate into her mouth.

"The Fairy Code Book!" Raina screamed. "It is gone!"

Melli rushed to Raina's side. "How is that possible?" she asked. "You are never without the book."

"Maybe we left the book on the dock at

Gummy Lake?" Dash asked. "Are you sure you don't have it? You are always so careful with your books, especially the Fairy Code Book."

Raina curled her legs up close to her chest and rocked back and forth. Her red wings hung low to the ground. "I *know* I put the book back in my bag at Gummy Lake."

"The book couldn't have disappeared," Berry said calmly. "Maybe it's just lost."

"Books don't get lost by themselves," Raina said sadly. Berry was usually the one to say something cool and calming, but right now Raina thought her comment was neither one of those things!

"We have solved mysteries and problems before," Berry told her. "We can solve this one."

"This is supersour," Dash mumbled. "First broken candy and Mallow acting strange . . . and now a missing book."

Raina lowered her head. "I don't know," she said. "This is most bitter. I have never lost a book—ever!"

"You're right, Raina," Cocoa told her. "Books don't just disappear. We need to figure this out step by step." She tapped her finger to her chin. "I know! You need to retrace your steps."

Dash snapped her fingers. "Sweet peppermint! Cocoa, you're right!" She leaned down closer to Raina. "Think, Raina. What would Lupa do?"

Raina blew her bangs off her face. She took a moment and then looked at her friends.

"Lupa never had a mystery this dark," Raina said glumly.

There was silence as the sun slipped behind the Frosted Mountains. A chill was in the air as the day melted away. Berry took out her shawl and handed it to Raina.

"We shouldn't rule out anything," Berry said. "What we need to do is investigate.

Melli stood up. "I think we should tell Princess Lolli," she said.

"I don't want to worry her," Raina said. "I have to try to find it myself first." She couldn't imagine the disappointment on Princess Lolli's face if she had to tell her the treasured book was lost. She stood up and straightened her wings. "I'm going back to Gummy Forest. Maybe there is a clue to where the book is."

"What about Blue Belle?" Dash piped up. "She was at the lake too, remember?"

Raina smiled at Dash. "Reading those Lupa stories has made you a great detective! You're right, maybe Blue Belle saw something."

"Now we have to find Blue Belle too," Berry said.

Cocoa waved her arm around. "Did you

notice that it's very dark out?" She pointed up to the sky. "There's no moon tonight. We can't see a thing . . . let alone a clue."

Dash reached into her bag and pulled out a sack of mints. "Good thing you have a Mint Fairy friend," she boasted. She tossed the candies to her friends. "This should help us with our search. Sure as sugar, we'll find the book."

Each fairy snapped a mint stick in half, and a pale white glow lit up the dark night.

"Thanks, Dash," Raina said. "These glow-in-the-dark mints are a help." Raina tried her best to sound positive. But the truth was that no one knew what would become of the Candy Fairies or Sugar Valley candy if the Fairy Code Book got into the wrong hands.

All the Candy Fairies' secrets were in that book. Candy Fairies would be in danger if the book was taken by someone. As Raina took off for Gummy Forest, she couldn't help but think that the missing book, the broken candy canes, and Mallow's unusual behavior were somehow all related. But how?

CHAPTER 3

Gummy Glow

With Dash leading the way through the nighttime sky into the darkened Gummy Forest, the five friends arrived at Gummy Lake. Dash's mints had helped them all to see, but Raina worried the mint glow wouldn't be bright enough to search for the book.

When the fairies flew to the dock, Raina showed her friends where she last remembered seeing the Fairy Code Book.

Raina replayed the scene in her head. Her bag had been next to her the whole time she was feeding the fish. Could someone have sneaked over and taken the book out without her noticing?

Raina's disappointed face was hard to miss, even in the dim light. "Sour sticks," she mumbled. "I hoped the book would be right on the dock."

"Me too," Dash said.

Raina walked around and around. "I don't know what happened," she said. Tears started to well in her eyes, and she turned away.

Berry took charge. "Raina, Dash, and I will search the forest and look for clues," she told her friends. "Cocoa and Melli, you check the area around the lake."

"Maybe we can find Blue Belle, too," Dash said.

"We're sure to find something," Cocoa said, trying to sound hopeful.

Everyone agreed and broke off to start the hunt.

"Even though I was worried about Mallow and the broken candy, I still think I would have spotted a Chuchie or something out of the ordinary," Dash said to Berry as she flew. "Do you think it's really possible Mogu stole the book?"

Berry kept her eyes on the forest below. "I

hope not," she replied. "I am no master of the Fairy Code Book like Raina, but I don't think the book has ever *not* been in a Candy Fairy's hands."

"I was afraid you were going to say that," Dash mumbled.

Raina listened to her friends talk, then beat her wings faster. Flying skillfully through the trees, she stayed low in order to see the forest below.

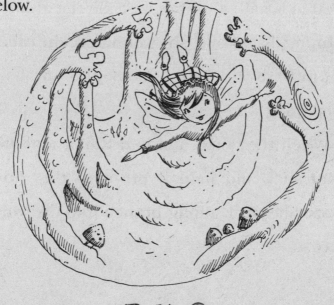

"Maybe another Gummy Fairy saw the book and picked it up for you," Dash said, coming up beside her.

Raina shook her head. "I thought of that, but any other Candy Fairy would know how worried I would be if I didn't have the book. Another Candy Fairy would have told me if the book was found."

As Raina rounded a gummy tree, she spotted a trail of white marks on the ground. "Hmm, what's that?" she wondered. She called out to Dash and Berry, "Come this way. I see something strange."

When the fairies landed, Raina took her mint stick and held it down to the white spots. She stuck a long branch into the white goo.

"Good gummy!" she exclaimed. "Is this marshmallow?"

Marshmallow in Gummy Forest was very unusual. While Marshmallow Marsh wasn't that far away, marshmallow was never seen outside the marsh.

"Sure as sugar, that is marshmallow," Dash said, kneeling down close to the gooey white mess.

"These markings in the marshmallow look like tracks," Berry said, bending down for a closer look. "But I'm not sure what kind of animal or creature made them."

Raina studied the funny shape of the imprints. "Let's check . . ." Then she stopped herself. "I was going to say we should check the Fairy Code Book."

"Let's report this discovery to the others," Dash said quickly. "I'm not sure what these marshmallow tracks mean or if they have anything to do with the missing book or what else happened today, but we have to let them know."

Raina bit her lip. If only she had her book to read about the tracks! Her mind raced through all the stories about different creatures and animals. Her head hurt! She just couldn't think straight. She felt Berry's hand on her shoulder.

"Come on," Berry urged her. "Let's see if Melli and Cocoa have found anything."

When the three friends returned to the lake, they saw Melli and Cocoa huddled around some gummy plants near the dock.

"Did you find something?" Berry called out.

Cocoa stood up straight. "We're not sure," she said. She pointed her mint candy to the ground so her friends could see better. "But there are a bunch of gummy plants around the dock that look like they were stepped on."

"And some melted gummy plants," Melli stated.

"Squashed plants sounds a lot like Mogu's doing. Do you think it could be a sign that that salty troll was here?" Dash asked.

Raina shivered. "I hope not," she said. "I can't even think what would happen if Mogu had the Fairy Code Book!"

"If Mogu did come here, I think he'd just be interested in the candy," Berry said.

"What would Mogu do with the Fairy Code

Book, anyway?" Melli asked. "He can't eat it."

"I wouldn't rule that out," Raina said sadly. "Mogu has an appetite for many things."

"Did you see Blue Belle?" Dash asked Cocoa and Melli.

"No," Cocoa said. "We called, but she didn't come."

"We found marshmallow by the old red gummy tree, with tracks in it," Dash reported. "They didn't look like the shape of Mogu's feet. And those tracks were much too small for a troll."

Cocoa raised her eyebrows. "Really? Marshmallow in Gummy Forest?"

"Any ideas about that? We thought it was very mysterious too," Berry said. "The tracks don't look familiar."

Raina sat down and rubbed her head. "Oh, I feel so confused. I just can't remember!"

Cocoa moved closer to Raina. "Let's see," she said. "We've got Mallow in Marshmallow Marsh awake during the day, broken candy canes, a missing Fairy Code Book, marshmallow tracks in Gummy Forest, and now a missing gummy cub!"

Raina wrinkled her forehead. "Blue Belle is always around here," she said.

"What does that all mean?" Dash asked.

"It means trouble," Raina said, rubbing her forehead. She slid down and sat on a gummy log. "Big trouble."

CHAPTER

4

Gummy Bear Clue

Maybe it's time we go to Black Licorice Swamp and talk to Mogu," Berry said. She looked at each of her friends. "If he has the book, we have to get it back. We must take charge."

Raina looked at Cocoa. Her Chocolate Fairy friend was the only one who had ever been to Mogu's home. She had stood up to the old troll when he had stolen her chocolate eggs. "Cocoa," Raina said, "what do you think?"

"I don't think we should make that trip alone or at night," Cocoa advised. "Black Licorice Swamp is very salty, and I don't think that I could have managed without Princess Lolli by my side."

"And we can't get to Princess Lolli," Melli moaned. She sat down with a thud. "This is not good."

"I don't think going to see Mogu is the answer," Raina said slowly. She stood up and began to pace back and forth. "We need to be *very* sure that Mogu was here before we go to the swamp. We can't blame him just because of some squashed plants. We need more evidence."

"Agreed," Dash said. "And sure as sugar, those marshmallow tracks aren't his." She wrinkled her nose. "We need to find Blue Belle."

"There is definitely a missing part to this story," Berry said. "There has to be another clue."

"I know it is getting late, but we can't give up," Cocoa told her friends.

Suddenly Dash jumped up. "I am going to go back to Mallow's tree right now. He might be there," she said. Her wings perked up as she spoke.

"But Mallow might be part of the problem," Berry pointed out.

Raina saw Dash's wings dip down. While she knew Berry was right, she felt bad for Dash. Mallow had to be part of this mystery, with his strange behavior. "Maybe Mallow will tell us something that will help us find the Fairy Code Book," Raina told her.

"You're right," Cocoa said. "The more information we get, the closer we'll be to figuring out this mystery."

"I'll go with you," Berry blurted out.

"Someone should stay here," Raina said. "This was the last place that I saw the book, so maybe we missed something. After all, it is dark out."

"Melli and I will stay here," Cocoa said. Then her face grew serious and her hands tightened into fists. "But if Mogu is the one who has done this, I am heading over to Black Licorice Swamp with or without Princess Lolli!"

Raina knew that once Cocoa had an idea stuck in her head, she didn't let go easily.

"We'll see," Raina said. "Don't dip your wings in syrup yet." She winked at Berry. "Come on, let's go see if we can find Mallow."

Just as Raina, Berry, and Dash were about to head off to Mallow's tree, Blue Belle appeared. She was out of breath and was waving her arms around.

Raina quickly went over to the young cub. She tried to soothe her, but she was frantic. "Calm down," Raina said. "Where have you been? We've been looking all over for you."

"Look how upset she is," Dash whispered.

"Shh," Melli said, straining to hear. The cub spoke in a hushed voice only to Raina.

"She has been looking all over for *me*," Raina

called over her shoulder to her friends. "She must have come while we were flying around searching for clues." Raina turned her attention back to Blue Belle. She pet the cub softly. "I'm here. You can tell me now."

The fairies stood quietly while Raina listened to the cub.

Finally, Raina gave the bear a sweet treat. She stood up and walked over to her friends. She took a deep breath and blew her long bangs off her forehead. Then she looked up at the dark sky. "Blue Belle says it wasn't Mogu who trampled the plants or tracked marsh-mallow through Gummy forest," she said.

"Well, that is a relief,"

Melli said. "Now we don't have to go to Black Licorice Swamp."

Berry moved closer to Raina. "If Mogu didn't make this mess, then I'm guessing he didn't take the Fairy Code Book either." She looked puzzled. "Well, who did Blue Belle see in the forest and at the lake?"

"Yes, who did Blue Belle say was here?" Dash asked.

"Mallow!" Raina blurted out.

CHAPTER 5

Gummy, Minty Mess

Raina saw Dash's face turn red. The Mint Fairy was never one to hide her feelings.

"There is no way Mallow made this mess and stole the Fairy Code Book!" she cried out.

"Now, Dash," Berry said, "don't get all minty. No one is accusing anyone."

"I am sure there is another side to this

story," Cocoa said. "We will find out when we find Mallow."

Raina rubbed her forehead. "This is turning out to be a supersour mystery," she said. She sat down on a hollowed-out gummy log. "I'm sure Mallow would never take the Fairy Code Book."

"We shouldn't jump to conclusions," Melli suggested. "Just because Mallow was up during the day doesn't mean he took the book."

"Hold on," Melli said. She held up her hand. "We need to hear if Blue Belle told Raina anything else."

Cocoa reached out for Dash's arm. "Melli is right," she said. "Let's hear what else the cub had to say before we go flying off to Mallow."

Raina took a deep breath. "Blue Belle says that she saw Mallow here at Gummy Lake earlier in the evening," Raina told her friends. "*Before* Sun Dip."

"Right after I saw him in Marshmallow Marsh," Dash said quietly.

"Now both Blue Belle and Dash saw Mallow during the daytime. It must mean something," Berry said.

I guess the question is, *why* was Mallow awake before Sun Dip?" Raina asked.

"And where is he now?" Berry added.

Dash looked over at Berry with an icy glare. "Mallow did not steal the Fairy Code Book! He could have asked Raina to borrow it!" she shouted.

Melli stepped between Dash and Berry. "Okay," she said, "we're all on the same side here."

Cocoa took out a pad from her bag. "I am going to start taking notes. This mystery is getting sticky."

"Blue Belle said that when she saw Mallow he looked like he was in pain. He was walking, not flying," Raina replied.

"Oh no!" Dash exclaimed. "He must have been hurt. Owls don't usually walk." She flew up in the air. "Come on. We have to go now and check on Mallow. We can't wait another minty moment."

"Raina, Berry, and Dash will go to the marsh," Cocoa said. She closed her notebook and handed it to Raina. "Hold on to this," she said. "Send Melli and me a sugar fly message as soon as you get any information."

"You do the same," Raina replied. She took

Cocoa's notebook and stuffed it in her bag.

With the mint sticks helping to light their way, Raina, Dash, and Berry wove around the trees and vines to Marshmallow Marsh.

"Who even knows if Mallow will be home," Berry said. "It is nighttime, and that's when Mallow is usually out and about." She paused. "Well, except for today."

They finally arrived at Mallow's tree on the edge of Marshmallow Marsh. Raina flew over to the owl's hollow-out tree and poked the mint stick inside. "Mallow?" she called. "Are you there?"

There was no answer.

Oh dear, Raina thought.

She was desperate to

ask him some questions . . . and find out some answers!

"I really didn't think he would be here," Berry said. She folded her arms across her chest.

"I hoped he'd be here," Raina whispered. Her wings dropped down as she came to rest on a branch next to her friends.

As the three fairies turned around to leave, Dash called out, "Look, there's Doopie!" She pointed to the trunk of Mallow's tree. The little red-and-white-striped mint chipmunk was rubbing her back against the tree. "She and Mallow are good friends. Maybe she knows where he went tonight."

"How strange that Doopie would be here in Marshmallow Marsh," Raina noted. "She usually doesn't stray from Peppermint Grove."

"This is turning out to be one minty night." Berry sighed.

Dash swooped down to talk to the small mint animal. But the chipmunk got frightened and scooted away, hiding under a nearby gummy bush. Dash tried again, a bit more quietly.

"Hello, Doopie," she whispered. "I won't harm you. Have you seen Mallow?" She held her mint up to Doopie's face.

The mint chipmunk looked up and tilted her head to the side. Her white stripes seemed to glow in the mint light. Dash noticed that Doopie looked a bit uneasy.

"Doopie, it's important," Dash pleaded. "I need to talk to Mallow."

The mint chipmunk backed away.

"Everything's okay." Dash tried to sound calm. "I am trying to help Mallow."

Raina flew down and stood next to Dash. She took Dash's hand. "I think Doopie is scared," Raina said. "She isn't going to answer you."

"But Doopie and I are friends," Dash said. "We see each other in Peppermint Grove all the time." Tears started to well in her eyes. "Doopie, please," she begged. "Please don't run away. I need to talk to you!"

The mint chipmunk raced away. She disappeared into the dark night in a minty minute. Now even her white stripes could not be seen.

"I scared her away," Dash said, crumpling to the ground. "Our best chance for a clue or an answer, and I scared her away."

"Well, I don't think we are going to find any more clues here now," Berry said.

"It's so late that we should just camp out here and wait for daylight and Mallow," Raina said.

"I'll fly and get some supplies," Berry offered. "I'll be back in a flash."

Raina looked out into the dark Marshmallow Marsh. This was one of the most bitter days she could ever remember. No Doopie. No Mallow. No Fairy Code Book. She was no closer to solving this gummy, minty mess.

And the longer the Fairy Code Book was gone, the worse it might be for all the fairies in Candy Kingdom.

6

Key to the Mystery

The sky was still dark when Raina opened her eyes. She couldn't sleep. Both Dash and Berry were snug in the sleeping bags Berry had brought, but Raina was wide awake. She wished that the pink colors of sunrise would appear across the sky. Once the morning light came, Mallow was sure to fly back home to his

tree. And when he did, Raina and her friends would be there.

Raina still couldn't believe that Mallow had anything to do with the mess in Gummy Forest and the broken candy canes—or the missing Fairy Code Book. She scratched her head. But there were still so many unanswered questions. She looked up at the hole in the tree where Mallow slept. She hoped he'd return soon.

Raina reached over to the small notebook next to her sleeping bag. She opened it and read the list of clues written on the first page. But she was so tired she just couldn't keep her eyes open. The letters on the page started to get blurry, and Raina rubbed her eyes.

"Raina!" Dash was shaking her shoulder. "Raina, wake up!"

Raina opened her eyes. The sun was high in the blue sky. She squinted and then put her hand up to block the bright light. "Oh no! I must have fallen asleep," she said.

Berry sat up. "We all overslept," she said. She stretched and tried to look inside Mallow's hole. "I can't tell if Mallow returned early this morning."

Raina flew up closer to the hole. It was in the shade, protected from daylight, and it was hard to see.

Raina wasn't sure if the owl was inside. She flew back down to her friends.

"What do you think?" Dash asked. "Do you think Mallow came back and we were all asleep?"

"It is possible," Berry said.

"It's hard to see in the hole," Raina said. "Maybe if I had some more light."

Dash took a large mint stick and flew closer to the tree with Raina.

"I am pretty sure I see Mallow's feathers," Dash said. "Double mint!" she exclaimed.

"I can't believe I fell asleep and missed Mallow's return," Raina said. Her wings were pointed down to the ground.

"Mallow holds the key to this mystery," Dash said.

"Maybe," Raina said. She glanced over at the dark hole in the tree. "Everyone knows you can't wake a sleeping owl. We'll just have to wait until Sun Dip."

"Humpf," Dash said.

Berry folded up the sleeping bags. "Maybe Melli and Cocoa have found something."

"Or maybe there's another book in Raina's library that can help us," Dash offered.

Raina hung her head. "No book has all the information the Fairy Code Book has," she said.

"That might be true," Berry said, "but we're going to get to the bottom of this." She stood tall. "We always pull together," she said.

"You're right," Raina said.

"I'll stay here," Dash offered. "If Mallow wakes up or Doopie comes back, I will send a sugar fly message right away. I promise."

"That's the spirit," Berry said, smiling.

Dash gave Raina a hug. "This isn't a short race to the finish," she said. "We're going to have to take on some sharp turns and falls."

Raina laughed. "I'm ready," she said. She took off toward Gummy Lake.

Raina saw Melli and Cocoa on the shores of Gummy Lake first. They were sitting on a bright orange gummy tree stump. Her friends' drooping wings told her that the fairies were still worried.

"I guess you didn't get to talk to Mallow," Cocoa said to her friends as they flew over. "When we didn't get a sugar fly message early this morning, we knew there was no news."

"Where's Dash?" Melli asked.

"Dash stayed at Marshmallow Marsh in case Mallow wakes up or Doopie shows up," Berry explained.

"Doopie? The little mint chipmunk?" Melli asked. "What is she doing in Marshmallow Marsh?"

"We saw Doopie by Mallow's tree, but she ran away before we could ask her," Raina explained. She handed Cocoa's notebook back to her. "I wrote it all down here so we could try to piece the story together."

"This mystery is getting stranger and stranger," Cocoa said, fluttering her wings.

Raina sat down on the ground beside her friends. "We fell asleep before Mallow returned to his tree," she said. "Can you believe it?" She shook her head. "Of all the times to get tired!" Raina continued sadly, "I am so worried about the book. And I really don't want any other Candy Fairy in Sugar Valley to know that it's lost. They may start to panic!"

"We're going to try again later today," Berry said. "I'm definitely not a night owl! It is hard to stay up all night."

"We were thinking we could have Sun Dip at Mallow's tree so we can catch Mallow as soon as he wakes," Berry told Cocoa and

Melli. "Our best chance of talking to Mallow is to get him when he first wakes up."

Melli spread some food out before her friends. "Have some breakfast," she said. "I was in Fruit Chew Meadow this morning and picked these fruits."

"Tell them what you just told me," Cocoa urged Melli.

"Tell us what?" Raina asked. "What's wrong now?"

Melli sighed and finished putting the fruits out on a blanket. "Well, it's not much more than sugar fly gossip, I think," she said slowly. She looked over at Cocoa, who nodded to go ahead. "There is some buzz about goblins in Sugar Valley," Melli finally said.

The thought of goblins in Sugar Valley

made Raina gasp. Once before, the fairies had heard about the mischief goblins could cause across the Vanilla Sea by melting candy, but that had turned out to be a friendly, lost dragon. Goblins were *worse* than Mogu and could cause much more trouble.

"We thought of checking the marshmallow tracks to see if those were goblin tracks, but we don't have the Fairy Code Book," Melli went on. She glanced at Raina. "I'm sorry."

"You're right," Raina told her. "The Fairy Code Book would have stories about the goblins and how to deal with them."

Berry stood up. "We can't send a sugar fly message to Dash with this information. Those sugar flies will spread that gossip faster than jam on bread."

"We have to find Blue Belle first," Raina said. "She'll have to come by this morning for food."

"Send a message to Dash to return to Gummy Forest," Cocoa said. "We need to make a plan if these goblin rumors are true."

"Think, Raina," Melli said. "We've never seen a goblin before. You must remember some story that can help."

"Goblins are sticky creatures and move quickly," Raina said quietly. She closed her eyes and tried to recall the pages in the book that spoke of goblins. "They are greedy and like gooey candy." She opened her eyes and looked around at her friends. "And I am very certain that it would be dangerous to all Candy Fairies if they ever got the Fairy Code Book."

CHAPTER

7

A Looooong Day

Dash's hand covered her gaping mouth. "Holy peppermint!" she said when she heard the goblin news. "What are we going to do?"

"I don't know," Raina said sadly. She had spent all day trying to find more answers about goblins in one of her many books. Now that all her friends were together at Mallow's tree, she hoped the owl would wake soon.

"This is stickier than I thought," Dash said, settling down on the branch by her friends. "No Candy Fairy ever wants to hear about goblins." She narrowed her eyes. "Wait, why didn't you tell me earlier?"

"Melli heard the rumors this morning, and then we checked all of Raina's books," Berry said. "We didn't want to send the news with a sugar fly. We wanted to try to keep the news quiet until we knew for sure."

Raina saw that Dash was upset and flew next to her. "We spent the day trying to find books with information about goblins," she said. She hung her head. She was finding it hard to focus and remember details from the Fairy Code Book. This was so not like her!

"We have no time to rest!" Dash said, springing up into the air. "Who knows where the book is and who is reading the stories and recipes!"

"Dash!" Berry grumbled. "That is not helping!"

Dash flew down and landed next to Raina. "I'm sorry, Raina," she said. "I guess we are all feeling stressed."

"The longer the book is missing, the more I feel we'll never see it again." Raina dropped her head into her hands. "What will Princess Lolli say when she and Prince Scoop return to Sugar Valley? They will be so disappointed in me!"

"She'll understand," Melli told her. "When has Princess Lolli ever gotten mad at you?"

"I've never lost the Fairy Code Book before," Raina said, full of gloom. "How could I have been so careless?"

No one said a word.

"No one close your eyes," Raina instructed.

"Don't worry," Dash said. "I am not missing Mallow this time!"

As the daylight faded, there was rustling inside the tree. The five friends perked up, inched forward on the branch, and peeked inside the hole.

There was Mallow! He stood in the center of his home with his frosted white wings spread open. He blinked his wide blue eyes and adjusted to the dim light of the fading day.

Raina didn't want to frighten Mallow. She

had seen how being so eager had scared Doopie away. She held up her hand to her friends. She wanted to be the one to speak.

"Good evening, Mallow," she said.

"*Whooo, whooo.* Good evening," Mallow replied. He inched his way over to the edge of the hole and just sat.

Hmm, that's strange, Raina thought. She wondered why Mallow didn't try to fly out of the tree. But then she noticed that he seemed to be leaning to the right and one of his wings was not spread as far out as the other one was. "Mallow, are you okay?" she asked.

Mallow ruffled his feathers and tried to straighten his wing. Dash saw him close his eyes. It looked like he was in pain.

"You're hurt!" said Raina. "What happened to you?" she asked, moving closer.

"Oh, noooooo," Mallow said. He turned his head around.

"Please, let me help you," Raina said.

Mallow looked at Raina and sighed. "My left wing is hurt."

Raina nodded. "Yes, I thought something looked wrong with you. My friends and I want to help you. Will you let us?"

The owl blinked a few times and then spun

his head around to see the Candy Fairies lined up on the branch. He sighed again. *"Whooo, whooo.* Yes, I will."

The fairies took out the healing bag they had brought with them. After reading in one of the Lupa stories about having a first-aid kit handy, Raina insisted that they bring one to the marsh. Dash put some mint syrup on Mallow's wing, and the owl sighed.

When Mallow looked calmer, Raina leaned in closer. "Mallow, there have been many strange things happening near Peppermint Grove and Gummy Forest. We know Dash saw you in the middle of the day yesterday. And now we wonder how you hurt yourself."

Mallow, with his big round eyes, looked as though he might cry. He started to speak softly. "There was something crumpling out in Gummy Forest," he told them. When I went to see what was happening, I clipped my wings." He swung his head in a full circle.

"You can't *fly*?" Dash asked.

Raina knew this news was not easy for Mallow to share. And all her friends had the same aching feeling. Not to be able to fly would be the worst fate. Mallow must have felt embarrassed.

"Once I arrived home, Doopie brought me some mint filling to soothe my wound," Mallow said. "But it will take more time to heal."

"So that is why Doopie was here!" Dash exclaimed.

"Shh," Berry scolded her. "Let Mallow finish."

Mallow backed away a little. "There is more," the owl confessed. "The noises I heard were made by greedy troublemakers."

"What?" all the fairies said at once.

Mallow lowered his voice to a whisper.

"Goblins," he said. "Goblins have come to Gummy Forest. That's *whoooooo. And they took the Fairy Code Book.*"

Bitter News

Goblins in Gummy Forest?" Raina gasped. Her wings started to beat faster. "The rumors were true!"

"Oh, Mallow!" Melli cried. "Did the goblins hurt you?"

Mallow stood tall. "I could outfly a goblin even with a wounded wing," he boasted.

Raina knew the proud owl was very puffed up about his flying. "Tell us what happened," she urged him.

"The other night, I couldn't believe my eyes. I saw goblins in Peppermint Grove," Mallow hooted. "There were two goblins, and they were very careless. They broke many candy canes as they ran."

"I knew there was something strange about those broken candy canes!" Dash exclaimed. She slapped her hand on her knee. Dash flew over to a branch closer to Mallow. "Were you following the goblins when I saw you in Marshmallow Marsh?"

Mallow spun his head and nodded at Dash. "Yes," he said. "I didn't want to worry you. Goblins are sneaky and get around quickly.

I could tell that they were looking for something, and I wanted to keep following them."

"Gooey gumdrops! They must have been hunting for the Fairy Code Book," Raina said. The pieces of the mystery were starting to make sense. "I wish you had warned me that goblins were around, Mallow."

The owl sighed. "*Whoooo.* I thought that I could protect Sugar Valley, *whooo.* And now I have made things terribly sour."

Raina felt bad for the owl. She knew how he was feeling. Often she wished that she could solve problems without anyone's help. "Oh, Mallow," Raina said softly. "We all have to work together. Especially when goblins are involved."

Mallow looked down. "I should have told

you about seeing goblins in Gummy Forest, Raina," he said. "A thousand hoots of apology."

"No use being sorry now," Berry piped up. "We have a book to find . . . and some gooey goblins."

"I was afraid she was going to say that," Melli whispered to Cocoa.

Raina spread her wings. "They wanted the Fairy Code Book," she said, "and now they have it." She looked around at her friends. "They will try to make our candy . . . and surely they will ruin the crops."

"What makes you so sure?" Cocoa asked.

Raina twisted her hair around her finger. "I may be

fuzzy on all the stories in the Fairy Code Book right now," she said, "but I can tell you this. Goblins can't make candy on their own. They may have the recipes, but they have no magic."

"So why steal the Fairy Code Book?" Melli asked.

"With the book, they have a better chance of learning some secrets," Raina said. "Now the marshmallow in Gummy Forest makes sense. That is a candy mishap for sure."

"I guess the question is," Berry said, "can they learn to make the candy, even without magic? Or make existing candy sour?"

Feeling all eyes on her, Raina took a deep breath. "I am not sure," she said. "But sure as sugar, they can make a huge mess."

"*Whooo,*" Mallow said. "This is bitter news."

Raina's head was pounding. Now that she knew who had the book, she knew the fairies had to get it back—fast.

"Mallow, you stay here and keep the mint syrup on your wing," Raina told him. "My friends and I are going to head back to my library. Maybe I have another book on goblins that will help us with this case."

"Now she's sounding more like Raina," Dash said with a grin.

"Actually, it sounds like Lupa," Berry said. "Maybe Lupa has a case like this in another book?"

"I'm not sure," Raina said, thinking hard. "But sure as sugar, I'm going to look."

"We can outsmart those goblins!" Dash exclaimed.

"Hold on," Melli said. "I think we need to let Princess Lolli know what is happening, now that we know for sure that it's more than just rumors that there are goblins in Sugar Valley."

Raina knew Melli was right. It broke her heart. "I'll write a sugar fly message," she said slowly. "Maybe by the time Princess Lolli and Prince Scoop get home we'll have some good news."

"I'll let the Candy Castle guards know too," Cocoa said. "We should tell them to keep a lookout."

"Thank you," Raina said. She was happy that her friends were around to help.

"Let's come up with a trap," Dash said.

"Thinking like Lupa again," Melli said.

"I'm glad!" Berry added. "That's what we need. A good detective. But how do you trap goblins?"

Raina scratched her head. She closed her eyes and took a deep breath. "With something sticky," she said.

Melli's hand shot up in the air. "Caramel!" she shouted.

Raina laughed. "Yes, caramel—and lots of it." She nodded. "Yes, I think we can catch goblins . . . and get the book back."

9

Perfect Plan

At home and surrounded by her books in her library, Raina finally felt better than she had over the past two days. Now that she knew that the goblins had taken the Fairy Code Book, she knew what to research. The Fairy Code Book would have an answer, but there were other books to read. She reached for

Lupa Stories and opened the large book on the table. Her friends circled around her.

"Yes, of course," she said. She turned a few pages. "What a great idea!" Her mind was racing as she quickly read the story of Lupa and the goblins.

"What?" Dash asked. "Raina, tell us what you are reading."

Raina peered over the top of the book and smiled at her friends. "Lupa had to face goblins too," she said. "And she says here that caramel is the perfect trap. Goblins love the sweet, gooey treat, and it's the perfect glue for holding them still!"

"You just have to have enough," Dash said.

"If the goblins were trying to make gummy candy and got marshmallow," Raina said,

thinking out loud, "I think I know how we can trap them."

"How?" Dash asked. "Just think of all the candy disasters that could happen in Sugar Valley if the goblins keep this up!"

Raina felt her anger bubble up inside her. "Let's leave a trail of notes leading the goblins to the key to the Fairy Code Book," she said. "The trail will end with a caramel trap."

"I think we should add some candy with the notes to make things *choc-o-rific* and gooey," Cocoa added.

"Good thinking, Cocoa," Raina said. "No one is greedier than a goblin."

"Lupa would be so proud of all of us," Berry said.

"Well, she'd be proud if we catch the

goblins," Raina told her, "and get the Fairy Code Book back safely."

Dashed yawned. Her yawn made Cocoa and Melli yawn. And once Cocoa and Melli yawned, Berry and Raina yawned as well.

"It is late," Raina said. She looked at her friends and saw the tired looks in their eyes. "We need to get some rest, but first we must set the traps and make the clues."

"What should the clues say?" Cocoa said.

"I'll handle that," Raina told her. "You, Melli, and Dash fly to Caramel Hills for the caramel for the trap."

Raina saw the worry in Dash's eyes. A smile slowly appeared on Raina's face. "The goblins aren't Candy Fairies," she told Dash. "They won't be able to figure out all our secrets in one night. And that makes all the difference."

Dash fluttered her wings. "I'm glad that I'm a Candy Fairy!"

"Me too!" Berry exclaimed. "Now let's set up the trap and then get some rest."

Dash, Melli, and Cocoa sped off to Caramel Hills with large buckets to scoop up the gooey treat. Meanwhile, Berry and Raina thought of clever clues to get the goblins toward the trap.

"How does this sound?" Raina asked. "'If you want to know the real secret of Candy Fairies candy, follow this trail to Gummy Lake. A sweet surprise is there for you.'"

"*Sugar-tastic!*" Berry exclaimed.

If you want to know the real secret of Candy Fairies candy, follow this trail to Gummy Lake. A sweet surprise is there for you.

She pulled a few sugarcoated candies from her bag. "And a few of these left on the trail won't hurt!"

"A good way to a goblin is through his stomach!" Raina said, giggling.

For the first time since the Fairy Code Book was gone, Raina felt sure of herself. "I think this plan is going to work," she said to Berry.

Soon Melli, Dash, and Cocoa returned to Gummy Forest.

"You asked for caramel, and now you've got it!" Cocoa boasted. She proudly showed off full buckets of melted caramel straight from Caramel Hills.

"Mmm," Dash said, licking her lips. "There's

nothing as sweet as fresh, smooth caramel from the hills."

"Or as sticky," Cocoa said. She made a sour face as she tried to rub off the caramel stuck on her hands.

"This trap just has to catch the goblins," Raina told them. "Thanks for getting the caramel."

Working together, the fairies set the trap in the moonlight. They poured the caramel into a ditch near Gummy Lake and then spread wide gummy leaves over the top.

"Now the goblins won't see the trap," Berry said.

Cocoa hung a large piece of chocolate from a gummy oak on the other side of the

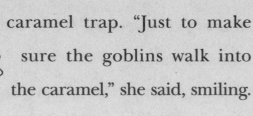

caramel trap. "Just to make sure the goblins walk into the caramel," she said, smiling. "Who could resist chocolate?"

"Hopefully not goblins," Raina said.

"Sure as sugar, we are going to catch goblins tonight," Berry said.

"Thanks for staying here tonight," Raina said as her friends settled into sleeping bags for the night.

"We wouldn't be anywhere else," Cocoa said. "I can't wait to see goblins."

"I can," Melli said, pulling her blanket over her face.

"There's no campfire, but could you tell a story?" Dash asked. She looked at Raina with her big blue eyes.

"There was once a fairy who had the sweetest friends in Sugar Valley," Raina began. She paused as she watched her four friends curled up in sleeping bags. "There was no greater treat for them than being together."

"Is this a story you remember from the Fairy Code Book?" Dash asked.

Raina grinned. "No, this is about my best friends," she said. "Thank you for sticking by me throughout this entire mystery."

"Now we just have to catch the thieves," Berry added.

Raina snuggled into her bed. "Yes, and we will," she said. "That is the sweet ending I'm hoping for tomorrow. Sweet dreams, and let's hope for a goblin catch!"

CHAPTER
10

The Catch

Raina woke up when the moon was high in the sky. Once again, she couldn't sleep. She wished that the sun would rise and the horizon would be a beautiful orange and yellow blend—just like the gummy flowers that grew by Gummy Lake.

Where are those goblins? she thought.

And then she heard a noise: a rustling in the woods. Raina knew it was time to see the plan in action.

She woke up her friends. Quietly and quickly they sneaked to their waiting spot. They stood behind a thick red gummy tree and kept watch. Raina wasn't sure how long she could stand to wait. She hoped the goblins had read the message and were following the trail to the lake. The trap was set, and the caramel was thick. They just needed the greedy goblins!

"Oh, I hope they come soon," Dash whispered.

"Me too," Raina said.

"Just thinking about all that caramel is making me hungry," Dash admitted.

Raina smiled. "I know," she replied. "After

we catch the goblins, we'll have a candy celebration!"

Just then there was some crumpling of leaves from behind the bush. Raina held her breath. She felt Berry squeeze her hand. She looked over at her friends. They knew this was the moment they had been waiting for. The goblins were close.

In a flash, Raina saw two goblins leap out of hiding and sprint for the chocolate hanging from the tree. Raina had never seen a goblin close-up before. She watched as the small creatures moved. They looked just like the pictures in Lupa's book: large ears and long faces, but no larger than a gummy cub. Suddenly Raina was not afraid. The goblins didn't look scary. They looked hungry! And greedy!

One of the goblins reached for the chocolate, but his skinny legs sank down into the thick caramel. The more the goblin tried to pull his foot out of the gooey mess, the deeper he sank.

The second goblin tried to help, but he got stuck as well.

The Candy Fairies couldn't help but laugh at the sight of the two struggling goblins.

"If they keep this dance up," Dash said, "they will make taffy!"

Raina and her friends giggled at Dash's comment.

"Who's laughing?" one of the goblins shouted. He held still and looked around. His small dark eyes darted around the moonlit forest.

Raina stepped forward with her friends close by her side. "You've been caught," she said. "We will let you out if you return the Fairy Code Book to us."

The goblins looked surprised to see the five Candy Fairies standing in front of them.

"How did you know?" the smaller goblin asked. He tried to move, but the sticky caramel held him back.

"We trailed your tracks and followed the clues," Raina said. "Your mischief-making is known all over Sugar Valley." She had never felt so much like Lupa! She spread her wings behind her and put her hands on her hips. "Where is the Fairy Code Book?"

"It's in his bag," the smaller goblin said. He nodded to his caramel-coated friend.

"I'll get that for *yoooooou*," a voice from above called.

Raina looked up and saw Mallow. The white owl swooped down, took the book from the goblin's bag, and dropped it into Raina's hands.

"Mallow!" Raina cried. "Your wing is healed!"

"Nothing like a little mint to heal a wounded wing," Mallow said, winking at Dash. He landed on a branch near Raina. "I couldn't miss this catch!" he hooted. "Greedy goblins always get their due," he said. *"Whooo, whooo!"* he cried.

"That book didn't help us," the larger goblin spat.

"It's useless!" the other yelped.

Raina nodded. "There is more than just words in the Fairy Code Book. Not everyone is able to create such sweetness."

"Raina is correct," Princess Lolli said as she flew down into the forest. She smiled at the five fairies and nodded to Mallow. "Prince Scoop and I got the sugar fly message. We hurried home, but I am glad to see that you have the situation under control."

"Sure as sugar," Raina boasted. She hugged the Fairy Code Book tightly to her chest. She looked over and saw Doopie and Blue Belle cheering by the red gummy tree. "Thank you," she called to them. "You were both a great help."

Princess Lolli faced the

goblins. "Gigi and Gion, you are not to take what is not yours," the princess scolded. "There are rules about this kind of bad behavior. You will need to report to Candy Castle so we can decide your punishment."

The two goblins hung their heads.

Princess Lolli waved her wand, and the caramel trap melted off the goblins. Two Castle Fairies appeared and took the goblins on royal unicorns back to the castle.

The princess faced the five fairies. "You were all very brave and quick thinkers," she said, "but you should never feel that you can't ask for help . . . even if I am far away."

Raina and Mallow shared a look. "When something as sticky as a marshmallow mystery happens, you need your friends to stick by your side!" Raina said. "I think we all learned that lesson."

"*Whooo, whooo!*" Mallow hooted loudly.

"For sure, I learned something very important," Raina told the princess. "The Fairy Code Book holds only part of the history. The secrets and the magic are within us."

"That's right," Princess Lolli said. She gave a hug to her Candy Fairies. "You have a greater power than you think," she told them.

"And I learned that friendship is the sweetest part of living in Sugar Valley," Raina said, looking at her friends. With her best friends gathered around her, Raina knew she was one of the luckiest fairies in the kingdom.

"Now that the goblins are gone," Dash said, looking around, "anyone up for a candy celebration?"

Raina laughed. "Sure as sugar!" she cried.

FIND OUT

WHAT HAPPENS IN

Frozen Treats

Melli the Caramel Fairy licked her fingers one by one. "Mmm." She sighed. "There's nothing like the warm, gooey taste of fresh caramel," she said. She looked over at a caramella bird perched on the tree above her. "I know you agree, right?" she asked. Melli dipped another finger in the barrel and lifted her finger up to the bird. "Let me know what you think. I am trying out new recipes for a caramel dipping sauce."

The yellow-and-white bird flew down to Melli's shoulder and pecked at the Candy Fairy's finger. The bird closed her eyes and flapped her wings.

Melli laughed. "I take that as a compliment!" she said.

She stirred the large wooden spoon around the barrel once again. "I think this is just *sugar-tastic* for dipping," she told the bird. "I can't wait for Sun Dip tonight. My friends will love this sweet treat."

"We don't have to wait for tonight!" Dash the Mint Fairy called from above.

Melli looked up and was surprised to see her four Candy Fairy friends circling the barrel. She giggled. "What are you all doing here?"

"We wanted to sample the new sauce!" Dash exclaimed. "How could we not try your dip?" The small Candy Fairy rubbed her stomach. "Any chance to try a new caramel treat!"

Raina the Gummy Fairy, Berry the Fruit Fairy, and Cocoa the Chocolate Fairy landed next to Melli.

"We wanted to come see you before you left," Cocoa added.

"Are you all packed?" Berry asked.

Melli shook her head. She was supposed to be getting ready for her trip to Ice Cream Isles, but instead she was too busy making the caramel sauce.

"We thought so," Cocoa said, giving a know-ing look to Berry. "We came to help you!"

"It's not every day a Candy Fairy gets invited to the Ice Cream Palace," Raina said proudly.

"And asked to make something for the Summer Spectacular," Berry added.

Melli knew her friends were trying to help, but she couldn't shake being scared about her upcoming trip. She had been so excited to get the invite to Ice Cream Isles from Prince Scoop, Princess Lolli's new husband. The prince loved caramel and asked Melli to introduce caramel dipping sauce at the ice cream celebration.

Melli was honored to be asked to contribute to the celebration, but she was also a little nervous about going on the journey alone.

"Is this the invitation?" Dash asked. She

picked up a sugar paper note. "Wow, this is *so mint*!" The invitation was a creamy vanilla color, with dark chocolate lettering. She held it up for the others to see.

"I've never been anywhere by myself," Melli said. "Every time I've left Sugar Valley, I've been with you." She looked around at her friends. She bit her lip and tried not to cry. "What will I do without you?"

"You are only going for a few days," Berry offered.

"And Princess Lolli will be there too," Cocoa said, trying to make her friend feel better.

"Princess Lolli and Prince Scoop would not have asked you if they didn't think you could do it," Raina said.

Dash flew next to Melli. "Plus you get to

take a royal unicorn ride on Butterscotch!"

"Even with the royal unicorn, it's a long trip to Ice Cream Isles," Melli said softly. "I'm really nervous. Plus, I won't know any of the fairies." She squeezed Cocoa's hand. "I wish you all were going with me."

"We wish we could be there too," Cocoa said.

Raina opened the Fairy Code Book. "Look at these pictures," she said. "The Ice Cream Isles are beautiful! You are going to love it there, Melli."

The fairy friends all leaned in close to look at the pictures. The swirling landscape was breathtaking.

"I bet the isles are even more beautiful than these pictures," Berry told her.

"Sweet Cream Harbor is full of ice cream

history," Raina said, reading the Fairy Code Book. "Swirl Island is in the middle of the harbor and is where Queen Swirl's great-grandfather, Sir Swirl, invented the soft, swirling ice cream."

"Sweet ice cream scoops!" Dash exclaimed. "You are going to have a delicious time."

Cocoa reached over and turned the page. "And look at the picture of the Summer Spectacular!" she said. "It looks like everyone is having such a great time at the ice cream festival. Sure as sugar, there will be new ice cream flavors to taste! What a yummy celebration!"

"Especially with Melli's caramel dipping sauce," Raina said, licking her finger. "Melli, this is delicious."

Melli did love looking at the pictures of the celebration.

"I'm sure you will make new friends at the Ice Cream Palace," Cocoa said. "You'll meet some really sweet Ice Cream Fairies there."

"What if they *aren't* nice?" Melli asked.

Raina put her hand on Melli's shoulder. "You are one of the kindest fairies I know," she said. "They will love you."

"Plus, you are going to give them a *sweet-sational* new ice cream sauce!" Dash exclaimed. "And you'll have to tell us everything about the Summer Spectacular and the Ice Cream Isles."

"Yes!" Raina chimed in. "I wonder how they make all those glamorous ice cream floats for the parade." She turned to another page in the Fairy Code Book and showed her friends the pictures.

"*So mint!*" Dash exclaimed. "The floats look delicious in the Sweet Cream Harbor."

"You are going to have *choc-o-rific* time," Cocoa told Melli.

"But I'm already missing you!" Melli said.

"We're here now," Dash exclaimed. "And I'd love to dip some of Cocoa's chunks of chocolate into that sauce."

Melli laughed. "Please, help yourself!" Melli could always count on Dash to have a snack. "I can't take this batch with me. I will need to make the sauce fresh once I am at the palace."

"No use having all this go to waste," Dash said, rolling up her sleeves. "Those Ice Cream Fairies are so lucky to have you come visit."

As the fairies started to dip their chocolates, Cocoa pulled Melli aside. "Being away from home is hard, but you'll be too busy to miss us. You'll have to make your caramel sauce. There will be so many new things to see and to do."

Melli hoped Cocoa was right. She glanced over at the picture in the Fairy Code Book. The Ice Cream Isles were beautiful, and the Summer Spectacular was a very important event, but she also thought the place looked cold and different from Sugar Valley. She just knew that it would be a little bittersweet to be away from home.

Candy Fairies

Chocolate Dreams

Rainbow Swirl

Caramel Moon

Cool Mint

Magic Hearts

Gooey Goblins

The Sugar Ball

A Valentine's Surprise

Bubble Gum Rescue

Double Dip

Jelly Bean Jumble

The Chocolate Rose

A Royal Wedding

Marshmallow Mystery

Visit candyfairies.com for more delicious fun with your favorite fairies.

Play games, download activities, and so much more!

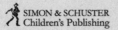